FLAT STANLEY's
WORLDWIDE ADVENTURES 11

Framed in
France

CATCH ALL OF FLAT STANLEY'S WORLDWIDE ADVENTURES:

The Mount Rushmore Calamity

The Great Egyptian Grave Robbery

The Japanese Ninja Surprise

The Intrepid Canadian Expedition

The Amazing Mexican Secret

The African Safari Discovery

The Flying Chinese Wonders

The Australian Boomerang Bonanza

The US Capital Commotion

Showdown at the Alamo

Framed in France

AND DON'T MISS ANY OF THESE OUTRAGEOUS STORIES:

Flat Stanley: His Original Adventure!

Stanley and the Magic Lamp

Invisible Stanley

Stanley's Christmas Adventure

Stanley in Space

Stanley, Flat Again!

FLAT STANLEY's
WORLDWIDE ADVENTURES BOOK No. 11

Framed in France

CREATED BY **Jeff Brown**
WRITTEN BY **Josh Greenhut**
PICTURES BY **Macky Pamintuan**

HARPER
An Imprint of HarperCollinsPublishers

Library of Congress Cataloging-in-Publication Data
Greenhut, Josh.
    Framed in France / created by Jeff Brown ; written by Josh Greenhut ; pictures by
Macky Pamintuan. — First Edition.
        pages cm. — (Flat Stanley's worldwide adventures ; #11)
    Summary: "Stanley Lambchop is whisked away to Paris, where he must help
catch a mastermind art thief at the historical Louvre museum by posing as a
painting"— Provided by publisher.
    ISBN 978-0-06-218985-1 (hardcover bdg.) — ISBN 978-0-06-218984-4 (pbk. bdg.)
    [1. Art thefts—Fiction. 2. Louvre (Paris, France)—Fiction. 3. France—Fiction.
4. Mystery and detective stories.] I. Pamintuan, Macky, illustrator. II. Brown, Jeff,
1926-2003. III. Title.
PZ7.G84568Fr 2014   2013032812
[Fic]—dc23   CIP
                                                                             AC

Typography by Alison Klapthor
14   15   16   17   18   CG/OPM   10 9 8 7 6 5 4 3 2
❖
First Edition

CONTENTS

La Mission Impossible

Stanley Lambchop stood before the map that his teacher, Ms. Merrick, had yanked down at the front of the classroom. She nodded at him to begin.

"I've traveled all over the world," Stanley told his class. "I've been to Canada, Mexico, Egypt, Japan, Kenya, and China." He pointed to each country as he spoke.

His classmate Molly raised her hand. "Do you always travel by mail?" she asked.

Ever since the bulletin board over Stanley's bed had fallen and flattened him, he had been easy to fold and mail in an envelope.

"Not always. Sometimes I fly," Stanley replied. He thought for a moment. "On a plane, I mean. Or I can float thousands of miles if the wind is right."

Stanley's friend Carlos raised his hand next. "So you've never been to Europe?"

Stanley turned and found Europe on the map. He scanned the countries that

made up the continent: England . . . Spain . . . France . . . Germany . . . Italy . . . "Actually, no, I haven't been to *any* of the European countries. . . . But I *have* been to *Australia*." He reached over, past Europe and Asia, and proudly tapped the country in the bottom right corner.

The map shuddered and snapped up like a window shade. All at once it was dark, and Stanley's body felt very tightly wound.

He'd been rolled up with the map!

"Hilph!" Stanley cried. He could hear his classmates laughing.

Suddenly there was a muffled announcement over the loudspeaker.

A moment later
Stanley felt himself
being unwound.

"Stanley," Ms. Merrick
said as she pulled the map
back down. "You are to
report to the principal's office at once."

"But it was an accident!" Stanley
pleaded. "I wasn't trying to be funny.
The map just snapped!"

"I know, Stanley," his teacher said gently. "I'm sure it's nothing serious."

Stanley slouched into the office, but the principal wasn't there. Instead Stanley found someone else—a man he recognized!

"Mr. Dart!" Stanley cried. "What are you doing here?"

Mr. O. Jay Dart was the director of the Famous Museum. Stanley had once helped him catch some art thieves. Stanley had been forced to disguise himself as a shepherd girl in a painting, which was very embarrassing. It was worth it, though, because he caught the thieves red-handed.

"Hello, Stanley," Mr. Dart said, quickly closing the door. "The principal was kind enough to lend me an office. I've come on official business." He laid a leather briefcase on the desk.

"Stanley," he continued as he turned the combination lock on the front of his briefcase. "Have you ever heard of the *Mona Lisa*?"

"The painting?"

"That's right," Mr. Dart said as the case unlocked with a click. "She was painted around 1505 by the great artist and inventor Leonardo da Vinci. When you see her, say hello for me, will you?" Mr. Dart winked mysteriously and lifted the briefcase's lid. A screen rose

from inside with a whirring sound.

Suddenly a dashing man with a polka-dot tie, thick eyebrows, and large, round glasses flickered to life on-screen.

"Stanley, I would like you to meet Agent Lunette of the Police Nationale in Paris, France," Mr. Dart said.

"*Bonjour*, Monsieur Lambchop," the man said in a thick French accent. He looked down his nose. "Eez it true you are v-air-y flat?"

Stanley nodded and turned to the side, and Agent Lunette whistled approvingly.

"Then you are the right boy for the job," Agent Lunette said. "The world's greatest art is going—*poof!*—into thin air, and only you can stop it!" His glasses made his eyes look very large.

Mr. Dart cleared his throat. "There have been a series of art thefts in Paris recently, Stanley," he said. "They believe the *Mona Lisa* will be next."

"Imagine! The *Mona Lisa* stolen from the Musée du Louvre, the greatest art museum in the world!" Agent Lunette cried. "We cannot let this happen!"

"He's right, Stanley," Mr. Dart said. "And as strange as it may seem, you are now a leading expert on museum theft. I've already spoken with your parents, and everything is taken care of. You'll be flying to Paris and staying with your aunt Simone."

Mr. Dart pressed a button, and the on-screen display split in two. "Staaaaaanley!" Stanley's aunt Simone squealed as she appeared on half of the screen beside Agent Lunette. Stanley hadn't seen his aunt since he was small,

but he remembered her bright-red lips and her stylish red hair, which fell in a slant across her face.

"Hi, Aunt Simone!" Stanley said.

"Let me see how you've grown!" she said, gesturing for Stanley to turn around. *"Mon chéri!* You are too thin! You must come to Paris and eat!" she crooned.

"I'm not too thin, Aunt Simone," said Stanley. "I'm flat."

"Come!" Aunt Simone repeated. "We will delight in the City of Light! The food! The fashion! The culture!"

Agent Lunette cleared his throat. *"Pardonnez-moi*, Mademoiselle. But Monsieur Lambchop cannot be seen in public in Paris. His presence will be a secret."

Aunt Simone huffed. "No, *pardonnez-moi*, Monsieur! My nephew will enjoy his visit!"

"No, no!" Agent Lunette snapped. "*Absolument non!* Absolutely not!"

"*Oui!*" Aunt Simone shouted back. "Yes!"

Aunt Simone and Agent Lunette glared at each other from opposite sides of the screen.

"We'll have fun, Aunt Simone, I promise," Stanley interrupted. "And don't worry, Agent Lunette. I'll keep a low profile."

Aunt Simone and Agent Lunette

both nodded grudgingly.

Mr. Dart glanced at his watch. "Your flight leaves in a few hours, Stanley. We'd better get you packed!"

Hello, Please, and Thank You

In an empty airplane hangar, Mr. Dart stood holding a floppy hat with a fur brim and a shirt with puffy sleeves. "While in France, you will be disguised as a member of King Francis I's court, as painted by the magnificent Renaissance painter Jean Clouet," he told Stanley.

Stanley blinked. "You mean I have to change *now*?"

"I'm afraid so," Mr. Dart said, handing Stanley the hat and shirt. "The only way to keep your arrival secret is for you to travel like any other priceless work of art."

Stanley changed his clothes, and a makeup artist powdered his skin and attached a beard on his face. When he was finally ready, Stanley climbed inside the frame. Because it was only a portrait from the waist up, he had to fold his legs behind the canvas.

Mr. Dart stepped back and looked Stanley over. "Clouet painted all the most important people in France during the early sixteenth century," he said. "But if I do say so myself, this may be his best work."

Mr. Dart carefully lifted Stanley's frame and laid it in a wooden crate. The crate had airholes and was filled with shredded paper for comfort. "Your mother has sent a cheese sandwich, some celery sticks, a bag of pretzels, and a juice box for your trip," he said, placing a small bag in Stanley's hand. "Also, here is a French dictionary and a book light. Good luck, Stanley."

"Thank you, Mr. Dart."

Then Mr. Dart closed the crate tightly, and Stanley's adventure began.

It was a little bumpy when Stanley was loaded onto the plane, but then

the crate came to a rest. Soon he heard the roar of the airplane's engines, and everything tilted upward. The plane had taken off.

Stanley switched on the book light and opened the French dictionary. He heard his mother's voice in his head. "The three most important phrases in any language are *hello, please,* and *thank you,*" she had once told him. "A polite visitor is a welcome one."

Stanley turned to the *H*s and found the word *hello.* He already knew that one: *bonjour.*

Please was harder. Stanley frowned. The French phrase seemed like a strange jumble of letters: *s'il vous plaît.*

Was it "sill vows plate"? But then he read that it was pronounced quite simply: "see voo play." "See voo play," Stanley repeated.

And finally *thank you.* *"Merci,"* Stanley said, stressing the "ee" sound on the end.

"Bonjour, s'il vous plaît, merci," Stanley said over and over, until he became very sleepy.

Stanley awoke with a jolt as the plane touched down on the runway. Before long he heard French voices and was suddenly jostled around as the crate was lifted and carried off the plane. After a few minutes—and a bumpy ride—the crate was set down again.

The top was pried off, and Stanley squinted in a sudden glare of morning light coming in through the window. He was in a bare room at the airport. Staring down at him was an officer in uniform.

"*Bonjour!*" Stanley said brightly.

The officer jumped. "The art, it talks!" He gasped, staggering backward.

Agent Lunette stepped in front of the man.

"*Bonjour*, Monsieur Lambchop," Agent Lunette said. "Please excuse my associate. He has never seen a painting like you before." He shook Stanley's hand.

Aunt Simone muscled Agent Lunette aside. "Stanley!" She bent down and kissed Stanley on one cheek and the other.

"*Bonjour*, Aunt Simone!" said Stanley. "Will you help me out of my frame, *s'il vous plaît*?"

His aunt carefully slid him out of his frame and stood him on solid ground.

"*Merci!*" Stanley said, happy to have used his third French phrase. But all of a sudden his legs felt funny, and he slumped to the floor.

"What is wrong?" Aunt Simone shrieked.

"My legs must have fallen asleep," Stanley said. "I've had them folded behind me for the whole trip. I just need to bend them back and forth for a minute, and then I'll be able to stand up."

Aunt Simone looked horrified. "This is how you welcome your guests?" she said to Agent Lunette as Stanley stretched. "By putting them in a box until they turn to mush?"

"Madame," said Agent Lunette. "We had to transport Monsieur Lambchop in this way to keep his mission a secret."

Aunt Simone wagged her finger. "It is against the Rights of Man! It is a crime!"

"*Non!*" Agent Lunette protested.

"*Oui!*" Aunt Simone said.

Stanley sprang up in between his aunt and Agent Lunette. *"S'il vous plaît!"* he said. His legs were awake now. "I'm okay. Really."

They glared at each other over Stanley's head. Then his aunt turned away in a huff.

"The Louvre opens in a few hours," Agent Lunette said, recovering his composure. "We have prepared breakfast for you here, and then we will depart for the museum."

"*Merci,*" Stanley said. "I'm starving!"

"Madame, will you join us?" Agent Lunette said, turning toward Aunt Simone.

Aunt Simone scowled at him then slowly nodded, reluctantly following them into the next room. There was a small table set with a white tablecloth. At each place setting was a plate with several rolls of different shapes and sizes, a boiled egg in a small cup, and a glass of orange juice. In the center was a bowl of fresh fruit, a vase of flowers, and crystal salt and pepper shakers.

After sitting down and putting his napkin on his lap, just as his mother had taught him, Stanley took a rectangular roll and bit into it. It was warm and light and buttery and sweet all at the same time—and in the center was a pocket of gooey chocolate.

Stanley closed his eyes and slumped back against his chair. It was the most marvelous thing he'd ever eaten—except, perhaps, for La Abuela's secret ingredient, which he'd learned how to prepare in Mexico.

"What *is* this?" said Stanley in a daze.

"Pain au chocolat," Aunt Simone said. "Bread with chocolate."

"It's so delicious," cooed Stanley.

Agent Lunette and Aunt Simone exchanged small smiles.

"This is France," Aunt Simone said. "Everything is delicious."

Hanging in the Louvre

After breakfast it was time for Stanley to climb back into his painting. Agent Lunette repacked him in his crate, but at Aunt Simone's insistence, the top of the crate was only gently shut. This meant Stanley was able to raise the lid a tiny bit and peek out as Agent Lunette and the other officer carried him toward the Louvre.

They were walking by a giant modern glass pyramid in the courtyard of a very large, old, important-looking building.

"The Louvre is one of the greatest art museums in the world," Agent Lunette said in a low voice. "More than eight million people from all over the globe visit each year."

They passed by a line of security guards and entered the building.

"The thieves have targeted the finest museums in Paris. Centre Georges Pompidou. Musée d'Orsay. One after the other, their most famous paintings have been stolen in broad daylight, during museum hours."

"But how?" Stanley whispered as they passed a statue of a sphinx the size of a lion. Now they were walking past a series of mummies. Stanley hadn't seen one of those since he'd been to Egypt.

"We do not know," Agent Lunette said. A statue of a woman with wings but no head towered over them. "They were swapped with fakes, without anyone noticing until it was too late."

They walked through hall after hall lined with paintings in gold-colored frames and filled with glowing faces against dark backgrounds.

Finally Agent Lunette and the other officer set the crate down gently. "Because of the thefts, all museums in Paris are closing early. The Louvre will close at three o'clock this afternoon. You will guard the *Mona Lisa* until then."

Agent Lunette carefully lifted

Stanley's frame and peered into his eyes. "You are a spy here, Monsieur Lambchop," he whispered. "Do not give yourself away. Do not smile. Do not sneeze. Do not move a muscle. You are a great painting by a Renaissance master. Act like it."

"Absolument!" said Stanley, pulling himself up straighter as he said his fourth French phrase. Agent Lunette hung him carefully on the wall and stepped back to assess the painting. Then he moved forward and straightened Stanley's frame.

"Très bien," he said. "That means 'very good.'"

He turned to walk away. "If by some

35

chance you are stolen, do not panic," Agent Lunette murmured. "We will find you eventually."

Stanley's eyes widened. "What?"

Agent Lunette looked at his watch. "The museum opens in three minutes and will remain open until three o'clock. After that, you will be able to stretch your legs before returning to your aunt's for dinner at seven. *Bonne chance,* Monsieur Lambchop." And then he translated: "Good luck." He marched out of the room without another word.

Stanley adjusted his arms and was freezing himself into position when he looked up and saw her. Directly across from him, on the opposite wall of the gallery, was the most famous painting of all: the *Mona Lisa*.

It was much smaller than Stanley had expected—no larger than one of the big art books his parents kept in the living room. But even from here, he could see her face: She had the slightest trace of a smile, as if she knew a secret. Her hands were folded calmly before her.

"Mr. Dart says *bonjour*," Stanley whispered.

Moments later the gallery began filling with people. Stanley quickly made his face a blank. A crowd gathered around the *Mona Lisa*, with many people jostling one another to take a photograph of her. Stanley kept his eyes trained on her smile.

It wasn't easy. Every time someone came close to Stanley's painting, he grew terribly nervous.

A group of Asian tourists talked excitedly about his painting for a long time. They must know I'm a fake! he thought.

A man in dark sunglasses studied Stanley's frame. He's plotting to steal me! thought Stanley.

A little girl pointed right at him. She can see my heart beating! thought Stanley.

But eventually everyone moved on to the next painting. Hundreds of people from all over the world walked by. Some barely glanced at Stanley. Some studied him silently for minutes on end.

Hours passed. Stanley grew tired. *Mona Lisa* continued to smile her mysterious smile.

Then a pair of young men walked up and stood in front of Stanley. One said, "Here's another one! Why is everyone in these paintings so serious?"

"Yeah," said the other. "It's like the *Mona Lisa* is the only one with a sense of humor around this place."

Stanley imagined the *Mona Lisa* bursting into laughter. And in that moment he was overcome by an emotion far worse than nervousness or boredom.

Oh no! he thought. I'm getting the giggles!

He bit the inside of his lip.

A woman with an English accent observed Stanley's painting and dryly told her husband, "This painting is more lifelike than you are."

Stanley's sides ached from holding in laughter.

Then a pair of French girls about his age came up to look at him. They were wearing school uniforms. The one on the right had big blue eyes and shiny dark hair pulled back in a ponytail. She tilted her head, looked at Stanley's face, and murmured something to her friend. They both burst out laughing.

At that moment Stanley couldn't help himself! A loud guffaw escaped his lips!

The girls gasped in shock.

An Artist's Eye

Stanley froze quickly. His face went slack. His eyes focused on *Mona Lisa*'s smile.

The girls stared, their mouths hanging open. One of them imitated the sound of Stanley's momentary burst of laughter. They giggled and whispered to each other.

Suddenly their teacher appeared

behind them. She was a tall spidery woman in a long black dress. She said something quick and stern in French. The girls looked at the floor and mumbled apologetically.

One of the girls went across the gallery to the *Mona Lisa*. The girl with blue eyes stayed where she was, pulled out a sketchbook, peered up at Stanley intently, and started drawing.

Stanley had never seen a person concentrate so hard. As she worked

with her pencil and eraser, feelings blew across the girl's face like seasons: She was disappointed, then frustrated, and finally pleased.

Stanley was very, very curious: What did her drawing look like? Did it look like him?

After nearly an hour, the girl paused. She held the book at arm's length, judging her work. Stanley's curiosity got the best of him, and he peeled his head forward to see.

The girl looked up, and he immediately snapped back into place.

Her big blue eyes narrowed. She took a step forward, studying him more closely than ever.

Stanley didn't dare move. The *Mona Lisa* was smiling as if she knew what a fool he'd been.

Then the strict teacher's voice barked something, and the girl snapped to attention. She fumbled to put away her pencil and sketchbook.

A guard by the door made an announcement, and people started exiting the gallery. The museum was closing!

The girl crept close to Stanley's painting. *"Au revoir,"* she whispered, and rushed out after her classmates. As she did, her sketchbook, which she'd shoved into a pocket of her satchel, fell out and onto the floor.

Stanley almost called out after her, but he caught himself. Soon the gallery was empty.

When he was sure the coast was clear, Stanley slipped from his frame and dropped to the floor. Creeping over to the girl's sketchbook, he picked it up, opened it, and found page after page of sketches—one painting after another, drawn in fine detail. There was even one of the *Mona Lisa*. Finally Stanley came to the girl's latest sketch.

Stanley was impressed. It looked just like him, except with a beard and a floppy hat. The girl with big blue eyes was very, *very* talented.

He turned back to the front cover. It read:

Le livre du
Etoile Dubois

L'école d'Art
22 rue d'Excaver
Montmartre, Paris

Her name is Etoile, Stanley realized. I have to return this to her!

Stanley looked up at the *Mona Lisa*. No one had tried to steal her . . . yet. She was safe for the night. Surely it would be okay for Stanley to stretch his legs after hanging on the wall all day—as long as he stayed in disguise and was back at his aunt's in time for dinner?

Stanley crept through the museum, moving silently along the walls and floors. He slipped behind one guard, and then another. He passed paintings by artists with names like Degas and Caravaggio. Stanley slithered down a staircase. He passed the pale bust of a woman whose arms had broken off; a sign said she was called *Venus de Milo*.

Finally Stanley found his way back to the front of the museum. The last of the visitors were leaving, and he caught a glimpse of a girl in a school uniform and a dark ponytail walking out the front doors—Etoile!

Stanley slipped into the coatroom. In a corner he found a large cardboard box labeled *Perdus et Trouvés*. Inside was a jumble of items, including clothing, umbrellas, and hats. This must be the lost and found, Stanley realized. He rummaged through the box and found a trench coat, a scarf, a dark hat, gloves, and tall boots. The coat and the boots were a little big, but Stanley felt that his shape was

well hidden. He found a box of tissues and took off his beard and makeup. Then he put Etoile's sketchbook in the coat's pocket.

He walked out of the coatroom, across the lobby, and into the sunshine.

Etoile was nowhere to be seen. Stanley found himself staring out at a river, which ran like a giant stone-lined canal through the center of the city. If he looked to his left, he saw a grand cathedral in the distance. He glanced right and saw the Eiffel Tower far away on the opposite bank. He looked down at the sketchbook. *Montmartre, Paris.* But which way was Montmartre?

As Stanley started walking, a sweet odor wafted through the air. At a nearby street cart, a jolly man in a cap was making razor-thin pancakes on a round griddle, topping them with fruit or chocolate. The smell hypnotized Stanley. His stomach grumbled, and he realized he hadn't eaten anything since breakfast.

"Une crêpe?" the man offered.

Stanley suddenly remembered Chef Lillou, the famous French chef who had plotted to steal La Abuela's secret ingredient in Mexico. In a fit of rage, he'd called Stanley a "crêpe." For the first time, Stanley understood why: A crêpe was even flatter than he was!

Stanley pulled out the pockets of his

overcoat to show that he had no money. The man shrugged, slathered a crêpe in fresh strawberries and cream, folded it up, and handed it to Stanley.

"Merci!" said Stanley gratefully. Then he held up Etoile's book and pointed to the address on the cover. *"S'il vous plaît?"* he said.

"Ah, Montmartre!" the man said. He pointed in the distance and made the shape of a tent with his fingers: a hill, that way.

Stanley said *merci* again and hurried on his way.

A Fresh Canvas

Winding his way through the streets of Paris, Stanley finally found a grand stone building in a maze of cobblestoned streets. The sign above the doorway read *L'école d'Art*, the same words that were on the sketchbook.

Stanley pushed open the giant door. Once inside he realized what *l'école d'art* meant: It was an art school. He

L'école d'Art

crept down a dimly lit hallway lined with empty classrooms until he came to one at the end, where he spotted the spidery teacher from the museum through the door's window. Inside, a handful of students were painting.

Stanley scanned the room. . . . There was Etoile, painting near the back! He'd found her! Now all he needed to do was find a way to return her sketchbook.

Stanley quickly removed his scarf,

hat, boots, and gloves. The less he wore, the more invisible he could make himself when he snuck inside. He even pulled off the puffy-sleeved shirt from the painting, so he was wearing only a white undershirt and his pants. He folded everything into a neat pile and hid it behind a trash bin in the corner of the hall.

Then, holding nothing but Etoile's sketchbook, he slipped beneath the closed door.

Stanley stayed low, skirting the edge of the room until he was directly behind Etoile. She was painting a young woman bending over a piece of lace she was mending. It reminded Stanley of one of the paintings he'd seen at the Louvre.

When the teacher's back was turned, Stanley popped up between Etoile and her painting. Her big blue eyes widened in surprise, but she stayed quiet. Then her eyes darted across the room—she was clearly worried that Stanley would get caught. As the teacher looked their way, Stanley quickly handed Etoile her sketchbook and folded his head and arms back behind her easel so his white T-shirt looked like a blank canvas itself.

Etoile immediately started painting on him. Stanley tried not to giggle as

she gently dabbed her brush against his chest.

Fifteen minutes later Stanley held his breath as the teacher came to look at Etoile's painting.

"*Très bien,* Etoile," the teacher said in an unusually soft voice. Stanley remembered that meant "very good."

Soon class was dismissed. Etoile said something to her teacher in French as the other students filed out—Stanley guessed that she was saying she wanted to finish her painting. The teacher left, closing the door behind her. And then they were alone.

Etoile said something excitedly in French.

Stanley rose up and shook his head. "I don't understand a word you're saying," he told her.

She grinned and poked his shoulder. "You were in the painting at the Louvre!" she said in English.

Stanley gulped. His mission was supposed to be a secret! "How do *you* know?"

The girl gestured at Stanley's T-shirt. He looked down and saw that she had perfectly re-created his painting.

"Who *are* you?" she said, her blue eyes dancing.

"My name is Stanley," he replied.

"I knew it!" she said, throwing up her hands. "I told my friend Martine you looked like Stanley Lambchop, the famous flat boy!"

Stanley felt himself blushing: Etoile knew who he was! "You dropped your book," he said. "I thought you would want it. You're a really good artist, you know."

Now it was the girl's turn to blush. "Madame Sévère would have been very angry if I had lost it. Thank you for returning it to me." Then she said, "What are you doing in a painting in Paris, anyway?"

"Uh, j-j-j-just visiting," Stanley stammered. He couldn't let on that he was a spy!

Etoile raised an eyebrow in disbelief. "Well," she said, "at least let me give you a tour of Paris. As a way of saying *merci*."

Beautiful City

"This neighborhood, Montmartre, has been home to great artists for centuries," Etoile told Stanley after he had put his puffy-sleeved shirt and trench coat back on and they returned to the street. "Claude Monet painted here. So did Pablo Picasso and Vincent van Gogh."

"Do you want to be an artist when

you grow up?" Stanley asked.

"I am an artist already," Etoile said. "L'école d'Art is a special boarding school for artists. Madame Sévère says the only way to paint like the masters is to copy them. Every day we go to a different museum to draw the paintings. And then we come back to our classroom and paint."

They walked down the hill of Montmartre, passing the famous Basilica of the Sacré-Coeur. As they wandered the streets of Paris, Etoile explained how the city was laid out in a series of rings, one inside the other. In the center was the neighborhood around the Louvre.

While they walked, Etoile asked

about Stanley's travels. He told her about performing with the Flying Chinese Wonders and jumping from a plane over Africa. He asked her questions about herself. *Etoile* meant "star." She had grown up in a seaside town in the south of France. Sometimes she missed her family. Stanley knew just how she felt.

Etoile and Stanley browsed the bookstalls on the Left Bank of the river Seine. In honor of his travels, Etoile bought Stanley an English copy of *Around the World in Eighty Days* by Jules Verne, one of France's greatest writers.

Then they visited the grand cathedral

Notre Dame, which Stanley had seen in the distance when he'd first exited the Louvre. It had gargoyles peering down from two huge towers and a colorful, round stained-glass window that stretched thirty feet across. The cathedral was nearly eight hundred years old!

Finally Etoile took him to the Eiffel

Tower. They rode an elevator to the top
and looked out over the city.

Stanley had never been anyplace that was so full of art and beauty. "How do you say 'beautiful' in French?" he whispered.

Etoile looked at him with her big blue eyes. *"Belle,"* she whispered.

"Belle," Stanley repeated softly.

Suddenly Stanley was startled by a shout. *"Arrête!"* a familiar voice called. "Stop right there!"

From the elevator behind them leaped Agent Lunette. "I've been all over the city looking for you!" He put a firm hand on Stanley's shoulder. "You are late for dinner!" he said in Stanley's ear. "Let's go."

Stanley's heart lurched. He was about

to protest, but Agent Lunette stopped him with a stern look.

Stanley forced himself to say, "*Au revoir*, Etoile."

"B-but Stanley—" Etoile sputtered.

"Please don't tell anyone you saw me," he said sadly. "I'm sorry."

Etoile's blue eyes stared back helplessly as Agent Lunette dragged him away.

Minutes later Agent Lunette and Stanley arrived at Aunt Simone's apartment. She shrieked when she opened the door.

"Stanley!" she cried, wrapping her arms around him. She examined his face. "Did they hurt you?"

"Who?" Stanley wondered.

"The thieves who kidnapped you!" Aunt Simone said.

Agent Lunette grimaced and cleared his throat. "Monsieur Lambchop was not kidnapped, Mademoiselle."

"I went for a walk," Stanley said. "I made a friend."

"A friend!" Agent Lunette huffed. "Monsieur Lambchop, nobody was supposed to know you are here. You have put the mission in danger! We found you only because we alerted the entire police force, and an officer at la Tour Eiffel recognized you!"

"You're right, Agent Lunette," Stanley

said. "I made a mistake. And I'm sorry I worried you, Aunt Simone."

Agent Lunette straightened his glasses. "Is there anyone else in Paris who knows you have come, Monsieur Lambchop?"

Stanley shook his head. "No. And I don't think Etoile will tell anyone."

"Let us hope not," Agent Lunette said. "Because tomorrow you must guard the *Mona Lisa* once more."

False Appearances

The next morning, after he dressed and his aunt reapplied his beard and makeup, Stanley hung alone in his painting. The *Mona Lisa* looked over at him with her sly smile, as if she knew all about yesterday.

Stanley still felt terrible. He had disappointed Agent Lunette and scared his aunt. And when he thought of Etoile, his stomach ached. She had looked so confused and hurt when he had been taken away. She had been friendly and generous, and now he'd probably never see her again.

Museumgoers came and went, remarking on Stanley and his painting. The *Mona Lisa* smiled her smile.

Suddenly there was a loud clattering, and all the visitors in the gallery turned to look. Even Stanley shifted his eyes.

But it was just someone whose camera had dropped by accident.

The murmur of the crowd resumed, and Stanley brought his gaze back to the *Mona Lisa*. But it took all his control not to furrow his brow. Something wasn't quite right. He'd never noticed the tree beside her head. And had she always turned her body at him that way? She looked back at Stanley with her—

Wait a minute, thought Stanley. She's not smiling!

The *Mona Lisa* had been switched with a frowning fake!

Stanley scanned the crowd for anyone suspicious but saw nothing out of the ordinary. Then he looked up.

There was a masked person, dressed all in black, sticking to the ceiling of the gallery. The person had suction cups on both hands and legs . . . and over their back was slung the *Mona Lisa*! The burglar was creeping ever so slowly toward the door.

"Stop!" Stanley yelled, reaching out of his painting to point to the ceiling. "Thief!"

The thief began scrambling more quickly. Agent Lunette burst into the

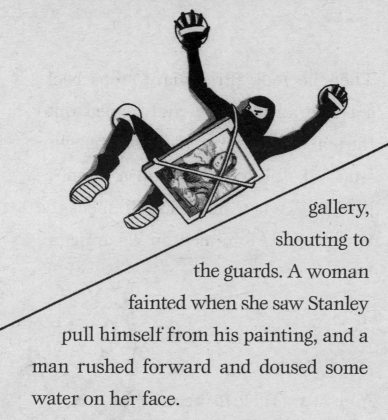

gallery,
shouting to
the guards. A woman
fainted when she saw Stanley
pull himself from his painting, and a
man rushed forward and doused some
water on her face.

"*S'il vous plaît?*" Stanley asked the man, pointing to the water.

"This is no time for a water break!" Agent Lunette shouted.

Without answering, Stanley splashed some water on his face and hands.

Then he took three giant steps back, got a running start, and leaped onto the smooth gallery wall. His damp skin stuck like plastic decals on a window, just like when he had climbed the Washington Monument in Washington, DC.

By peeling his hands off and re-sticking them a few inches ahead of him, he was able to creep up the wall and onto the ceiling. The thief stuck and unstuck the suction cups speedily to flee.

Stanley inch-wormed across the ceiling as the crowd watched below. When he had almost caught up, the thief looked back, unstuck their right leg, and brought their knee down hard on Stanley's hand.

"Argh!" Stanley cried out in pain. The thief lifted their leg again, and Stanley grabbed the suction cup and hung on to it with one hand as he dangled over the crowd. Everyone gasped.

The thief jerked around, trying to shake Stanley loose. But Stanley wouldn't let go. Instead he grabbed the thief's leg with his other hand and started swinging back and forth, stretching the thief's leg farther and

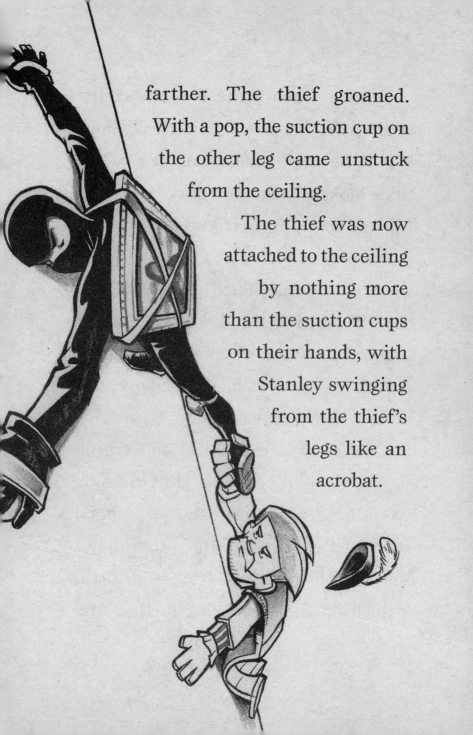

farther. The thief groaned. With a pop, the suction cup on the other leg came unstuck from the ceiling.

The thief was now attached to the ceiling by nothing more than the suction cups on their hands, with Stanley swinging from the thief's legs like an acrobat.

"Say *au revoir*," Stanley growled. He swung harder. With a squeak, the remaining two suction cups came undone.

"Nooooo!" cried the thief as they began to fall. Stanley swung up toward the ceiling as the thief fell down. He hooked his feet around the thief's shoulders. In midair, Stanley's body ballooned upward like a parachute, holding the thief beneath him.

They landed gently, with the *Mona Lisa* unharmed.

"You are under arrest!" Agent Lunette immediately cut the *Mona Lisa* from the thief's back and handed the painting to one of the officers. Then he pulled the thief's hands behind them and handcuffed them. Finally he pulled off the mask . . . and a short crop of dark hair spilled out.

Stanley sucked in a breath. "It's M-Madame Sévère!" he stammered. "She's a teacher at L'école d'Art!"

"As I tell my pupils," Madame Sévère said coldly, "the only way to paint like the masters . . . is to steal from them. My plan was perfect."

"No," Stanley replied. "Your plan fell *flat*."

All the museum visitors burst into applause as the officer led Madame Sévère away. Agent Lunette slapped Stanley on the back. "You have done it, Monsieur Lambchop! How can we ever repay you?"

Stanley thought for a moment. "There is one thing I'd like to do before I leave Paris."

Crêpe Stanley

Aunt Simone chose the restaurant for dinner: She said it was one of the finest in Paris. She wore a red dress to match her red lips and hair, and Agent Lunette was dressed in his best uniform, with medals pinned to his chest. Stanley had on a white shirt and a tie. When Etoile arrived, her dark hair was pulled back off her face. Her blue eyes sparkled in the candlelight.

While Aunt Simone and Agent Lunette talked to each other in French, Stanley leaned toward Etoile.

"Sorry I left you at the Eiffel Tower," he told her.

"I *knew* you weren't just visiting," Etoile said with a smile.

"Are you upset about your teacher?" asked Stanley.

Etoile's face darkened. "Madame made us copy masterpieces so she could have something to hang on the walls after she stole the originals. From now on, I will create my own masterpieces. Maybe one day they will hang in the Louvre."

"I hung in the Louvre for two whole days," said Stanley. "It's not as glamorous as it looks."

Etoile laughed.

Their meal was served, and Stanley remembered what his aunt had said when he first arrived: "This is France. Everything is delicious." He couldn't agree more. The beef Bourguignonne was rich and full-bodied, just like the province of Burgundy where Aunt Simone said it was a specialty. They agreed that the Camembert cheese tasted like the fields in the town of Camembert. There was cassoulet stew from Toulouse filled with beans and meat that made Stanley feel as if he were by a fireplace in a country castle.

"This is the finest meal I have ever had," Agent Lunette said. He looked into Aunt Simone's eyes. "And it is only partly because of the food."

Aunt Simone waved him away, but Stanley noticed her blushing. "Oh, Pierre, you are such a romantic!"

Stanley smiled. Just then the waiter appeared with the chef. "Monsieur Lambchop," he said, "the chef has something special for you."

Stanley looked up and nearly fell out of his chair. "No!" he cried. In his panic, he leaped up onto the table, grabbed a fork, and brandished it in front of him.

"Stanley, what's wrong?" cried Aunt Simone.

"The chef!" Stanley declared. "He's the one who chased me across Mexico, trying to steal La Abuela's secret!"

Chef Lillou held out his palms and shook his head. *"Non! Non! S'il vous plaît,"* he pleaded. "Please. I am not the man I was. I was wrong. I want to apologize."

"You— What?" Stanley said, surprised.

"I have dreamed of seeing you again. I am glad you stopped me in Mexico. There was a missing ingredient in my life. I thought it was La Abuela's secret, but I was a fool. It was only when I came back to Paris that I found what was missing. It was *amour*—love. Everything changed when I found my true love. *I* changed."

Suddenly the hostess of the restaurant, a plump woman with a warm smile, appeared and wrapped her arms around the chef.

"*L'amour* changes everything," she said.

Stanley didn't know what to say. Meanwhile, Agent Lunette and Aunt Simone were staring dreamily into each other's eyes.

"*Oui*," Aunt Simone said lightly. "*L'amour* changes everything."

"*Oui*," Agent Lunette agreed. He took her hands and held them to his cheek.

Etoile wrinkled her nose at Stanley. "Maybe you should get down off the table now," she whispered.

Stanley thought that was a good idea, so he did.

The waiter wheeled over a silver platter. "I have created a new dish,"

Chef Lillou announced. "All over the world, Crêpe Suzette is known as one of the great French desserts. But I have made something new. Something *magnifique*. It is called Crêpe Stanley!"

The waiter lifted the silver dome off the platter with a flourish, and everyone oohed and ahhed.

Stanley and Etoile were finally full after they'd each eaten eight entire Crêpe Stanleys.

"My compliments to the chef!" Stanley told Chef Lillou, shaking his hand. "Can I take some home for my brother, Arthur, too?"

Au Revoir

Etoile and Stanley stood together beneath the Arc de Triomphe, a giant monument shaped like an arch in the center of the city. The lights of Paris twinkled around them.

"I feel so small standing here," said Etoile.

"I feel flat," said Stanley, "like usual."

Etoile laughed. "Will you write

me?" she asked.

Stanley nodded. Then he said, "Maybe one day I can come visit by airmail."

"I hope so," said Etoile.

Neither of them said anything for a long time.

"It's time for me to go," Stanley said at last. *"Au revoir*, Etoile."

"Au revoir, Stanley."

She turned to walk away—and then she spun around and gave Stanley a hug and a kiss on the cheek. And in that moment, the evening breeze almost blew him away.

One afternoon, several weeks later, Stanley and his brother, Arthur, were

lying on their beds in their room, daydreaming of Paris.

Arthur groaned. "I would give anything to have one more Crêpe Stanley. I can't believe I ate all forty-six of them the night you got home."

"Why don't you write Aunt Simone?" Stanley said. "I bet she could get Chef Lillou to send you some more."

"Why don't you just climb in an envelope and go get me some more?" replied Arthur.

"Why don't I flatten you with a bulletin board and then *you* can climb into an envelope?" teased Stanley.

Stanley reached under his pillow,

and pulled out the latest letter from
Etoile. He never got tired of rereading
her letters.

One of her paintings had been accepted into a special exhibition of young artists' work. It was a portrait of him called *La Terre Est Plate*: "The World Is Flat." He glanced up at his wall. Next to his bulletin board, he'd hung the T-shirt he was wearing the day they'd met—the one that she had painted on. He thought it was a masterpiece. He tucked the letter back under his pillow.

Arthur suddenly jumped from his bed and onto Stanley's. "I know how we can make more," said Arthur with a devilish grin, towering over Stanley.

"Arthur, don't—" Stanley said.

"S'il vous plaît," Arthur said. "May I please have . . ."

"Arthur!" Stanley giggled.

Arthur leaped in the air and threw himself down on Stanley, rolling over his body like a rolling pin.

"Crêpe Stanley!" he shouted.

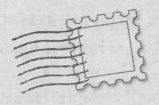

WHAT YOU NEED TO KNOW ABOUT PARIS

The Eiffel Tower was built for the 1889 Paris World's Fair. It was the entrance arch for the fair.

The Louvre Museum was built in 1190 as a fortress. It was rebuilt as a royal palace in the sixteenth century and became a museum in 1793.

France is the most visited country in the world, with over 80 million visitors per year.

The largest bell in the Notre Dame Cathedral weighs about 26,000 pounds!

The *Mona Lisa* was stolen from the Louvre in 1911. After two years, French authorities finally found the Italian thief and recovered the painting.

It took almost 200 years to finish building the Notre Dame Cathedral.

A replica of the Statue of Liberty stands on Île aux Cygnes, a man-made island in the middle of the Seine River, which runs through Paris.

France makes almost 400 different types of cheese!

The Tour de France started in 1903 and is the most famous bike race in the world. Competitors bike almost 2,000 miles all around France over twenty-three days.

Montmartre, a hill in the northern part of Paris, is the highest point in the city.

There's No Place on Earth
That a Flat Kid Can't Go!
Don't Miss:

Turn the Page to Read a Sample!

Caught in San Francisco

The hills in San Francisco were so steep that all the parked cars looked as if they were going to roll away. Stanley Lambchop was climbing the sidewalk alongside his old friend Thomas Anthony Jeffrey, whom the Lambchops were visiting on their family vacation.

"I can't believe how much has happened since the last time I saw you,"

Stanley said to Thomas as they walked with Stanley's parents and brother, Arthur, up the hill. "You had just moved to California, and it was my first time traveling by mail. I hadn't even been flat long enough to get creased!"

Thomas laughed. "I remember opening your envelope. You smelled like egg salad."

Arthur shook his head. "I told you, Mom: Egg salad and milk in the mail is a bad idea!"

"*Are* a bad idea," corrected Stanley's mother, who was a stickler for good grammar. "I didn't want Stanley to go hungry. After all, it was his first time away from home!"

"I remember thinking, *California, wow!*" Stanley went on. "I'd never traveled so far away. And to think, now I've been all over the world."

"You have had a lot of excitement," said Thomas. Then he added playfully, "Though you still kind of smell like egg salad."

"I do not!" cried Stanley, cracking up.

Since the bulletin board over Stanley's bed had fallen and flattened him, he had been to Egypt, Kenya, France, Australia, and lots of other places—but there was still something nice about exploring a city like San Francisco with his family and a good friend. Thomas had shown them Haight Ashbury, where everyone seemed to be wearing tie-dye T-shirts, and taken them on an old-fashioned-looking cable car to Union Square, where people in business suits hurried in and out of skyscrapers. Except for the moment at Fisherman's Wharf when a group of tourists had recognized Stanley and insisted on taking pictures with him, Stanley felt like a regular sightseer. Now they were heading to the Japantown district for dinner.

As they came to the top of the hill, Stanley suddenly heard a scream. He spun around to see a girl in a wheelchair barreling down the middle of the street.

"HELP!" the girl shrieked.

Stanley leaped into action. "Thomas, throw me! Quick!"

"What?" said Thomas, in shock.

But then Arthur stepped up, took Stanley's hands, and launched him into the air like a boomerang.

"Stanley, don't!" his father yelled after him. As the wheelchair zoomed past, Stanley caught the back of it with both arms. His body ballooned backward like a parachute, and the wheelchair slowed.

"I have you!" Stanley reassured the girl.

But then he felt a tug at his back. His father had caught up and grabbed Stanley's shirt.

"Stanley!" Mr. Lambchop gasped. "It's not safe!"

"Dad! Let go!" yelled Stanley. "I have this under control!"

With his father pulling on him, one of Stanley's hands came loose from the back of the wheelchair, and his body swung backward.

"Eek!" screeched Mr. Lambchop. Now they were all in trouble. It was as if Mr. Lambchop were waterskiing behind the speeding wheelchair . . . except there was no water and Stanley was the rope.

Now it was Stanley and his father's turn to scream, "HELP!"

Suddenly, the wheelchair came to a

halt. Stanley shot over the girl's head, and his father went flying after him.

They landed with a thunk in the open bay of a cargo van, which was parked at the bottom of the hill. The girl rolled up a ramp into the van after them. She appeared to be in perfect control.

"Let's blow this taco stand!" she called to the driver.

Suddenly the doors swung closed, and the van peeled away.

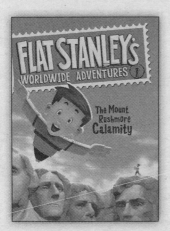